fimbles ™

Suitcase

CBeebies
BBC

Bessie flew past the magical Tinkling Tree and landed alongside her friends, the Fimbles.

"Hello!" she called.

"What are you making?"
"Paper plate pies for our picnic," said Fimbo.
"Picnic! Picnic!" squealed Pom. Baby Pom loved picnics.

"That apple looks good enough to eat," laughed Bessie, looking at the pictures.

"Apple! Apple!" said Baby Pom. "Please!"

"Are you hungry, Pom?" Bessie asked.
"I'll get you an apple," said Florrie, and went to find one.

On the way, Florrie's fingers started to twinkle.
"Oh, I'm getting the Fimbling Feeling!" she cried.

The branches of the Tinkling Tree began to shimmer, and its flowers began to tinkle.

The bubbles from the Bubble Fall
went "Ping! Ping!" and Florrie
couldn't help dancing
and singing the
Fimbling song.

"I can feel a twinkling,
I can hear a sound,
It's telling me there's something
Waiting to be found!
Where is it? Where is it?
What could it be?
I think it might be over there,
Let's go and see!"

"Look what I've found!" said Florrie.
"I wonder what it is?"
She bent down to take a closer look.

"Tickle my tadpoles!" said
Rockit. "That's a suitcase.
I bet it would make a
good drum."

Florrie banged the drum and Rockit did a rockity dance to the beat.

Florrie wanted to know what was inside the suitcase, so she opened it up.

It was empty!

Baby Pom and Fimbo came over to see what Florrie had found.

"Apple! Apple!" said Pom. She had hoped there might be an apple inside.

"Sorry, Pom. It's empty," sighed Florrie.

"You know," said Bessie, who had been watching them, "I think an empty suitcase is better than a full one."

"Why?" asked Florrie.
"Just think of all the things you can put inside it," said Bessie. "And all the places you can go with it."

"Find out! Find out!" giggled Baby Pom.

So the Fimbles decided to find out.

suitcase

"We could take our suitcase to the seaside," suggested Rockit.

"Oh yes!" said Fimbo. "Or the jungle."

"Let's take it on our picnic," said Florrie. "We can put everything we need in it."

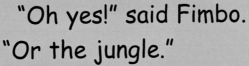

"Picnic! Picnic!" said Baby Pom.

As everyone packed the suitcase, they sang a song.

"Oh...we're going on a picnic, yes, we are," sang the Fimbles.

"Yes, we are!" echoed Rockit.

"I am packing things to eat!" sang Fimbo.

"Apples are my favourite treat!" sang Florrie.

"Picnic, picnic, picnic!" sang Baby Pom. She shook
Fimbo's Shimmy Shaker and put it back in the suitcase.

At last! The suitcase was packed with everything the Fimbles wanted for their picnic.

But Rockit couldn't close the lid – even when he bounced on it.

"There are too many things in the suitcase. Look! That beach ball is just too big!" Florrie said.

So Fimbo took out the beach ball.

But Fimbo and Florrie still couldn't close the suitcase. Fimbo liked the beach ball, so he put it back into the suitcase.

Just then, Roly Mo popped up.

"We're going on a picnic," explained Florrie. "But we can't close our suitcase."

Roly Mo smiled. "You need to leave some things behind," he said. "I know a rhyme that might help you."

"Eeny, meeny, miney, mo! Is it yes or is it no? Which will stay and which will go? Eeny meeny miney mo!"

Florrie went first and, as she said the rhyme, her finger touched a cushion in the suitcase.

"Who put that in?" she asked.

"I did!" said Rockit, and he took out the cushion.

Then it was Baby Pom's turn.

"Eeny, eeny, eeny, moooo!" sang Baby Pom, and her finger touched Fimbo's Shimmy Shaker.

Baby Pom took the Shimmy Shaker out. This time, when everyone tried to shut the lid...

...it closed!

"Well done!" said Roly Mo, and the Fimbles began to sing again.

"Oh, we're going on a picnic, yes, we are..."

"Yes, we are!" sang Rockit, loudly.

"Oh, no, we're not," said Florrie, out
of breath. "The suitcase is too heavy!"

Baby Pom had an idea. She fetched her Trundle Truck, and held it steady while Florrie and Fimbo put the suitcase on it.

"Well done, Pom!" said Fimbo.
Baby Pom pushed her Trundle Truck to the Purple Meadow.
Fimbo and Florrie unpacked the picnic things, and Baby Pom got an apple to eat.

"The Fimbles had a lovely time today," laughed Bessie as she cuddled up to Ribble.
"That empty suitcase was a lot of fun, after all!"